BROTHERS OF THE WIND

Barbara Berger
1982

BROTHERS
OF THE WIND

BY JANE YOLEN
with illustrations by Barbara Berger

PHILOMEL BOOKS   NEW YORK

Library of Congress Cataloging in Publication Data
Yolen, Jane.
Brothers of the wind.
SUMMARY: A slave boy runs away with a winged horse that
displeases his Sheik and presents the horse to the ailing Caliph
who puts off dying until the horse is old enough to ride.
[1. Horses—Fiction] I. Berger, Barbara, 1945
(Mar. 1)— II. Title.
PZ7,Y78Br   [Fic]   80-25562
ISBN 0-399-20787-2

Published by Philomel Books
a division of the Putnam Publishing Group
200 Madison Avenue, New York, New York 10016
Text copyright © 1981 by Jane Yolen
Illustrations copyright © 1981 by Barbara Berger
Printed in the United States of America.

CONTENTS

For Edie,
Arlene,
and the Sisters of The Elms

BROTHERS OF THE WIND

"Little brother, new and weak," he crooned, "we must go out into the sun. Do not fear the eye of God, for all that has happened, all that will happen, is already written. And if it is written that we brothers will survive, it will surely be so."

Then Lateef walked out of the tent.

THE DESERT

Lateef and the foal both blinked as the bright sun fell upon them. From the inside of the tent, the mare cried out, an anguished farewell. The foal gave a little shudder and was still.

But Lateef was not still. He looked around once at the village of tents that rimmed the oasis. He watched as some slave girls, younger even than he, bent over the well and drew up water. He had known them all his life, but they were still strangers to him. His mother had died at his birth; her mother had died the same way. He was indeed an orphan's orphan, a no-man's child, a slave of slaves. He would leave this home of familiar strangers with no regrets and take his burden—jest or test—out into the burning sands. He had thought about it, though thinking was not for slaves. He had thought about it and decided that he would stay with the foal. His orders were to take it out into the sands. And perhaps the keeper-of-horses expected them both to die there. But what if their deaths were not written? Could that be part of Allah's test? He would go out into the sands as ordered, and then turn north to Akbir. Akbir, the city of dreams. If it were written anywhere that the foal was to live, in Akbir that writing could be understood.

It was noon when Lateef set out and the fierce eye of the sun was at its hottest. It was a time when no son of the desert would ordinarily dare the sands. But Lateef had no choice. If he did not leave at once, he would be beaten for disobedience. If he did not leave at once his courage, what little there was, would fail him. And if he did not leave at once, some other slave would take the foal and leave it out on the desert and then the foal with wings would surely die.

North to Akbir. Lateef felt the sand give way beneath his feet. It poured away from his sandals like water. Walking in the desert was hard, and made harder still by the heavy burden he was carrying on his back.

He turned once to look at the oasis. It was now only a shimmering line on the horizon. He could see no movement there. He continued until even that line disappeared, until his legs were weak and his head burned beneath his *dulband.* Only then did he stop, kneel down, and place the foal gently onto the sand. He shaded it with his own shadow.

The foal looked up at the boy, its eyes brown and pleading.

"Only one small drink now," cautioned Lateef. He held the wineskin out and pressed its side. Milk streamed into the foal's mouth and down the sides of its cheeks.

"Aiee," Lateef said to himself, "too quickly!" He gave one more small squeeze on the wineskin, then capped it. All the while he watched the foal. It licked feebly at the remaining milk on its muzzle. Its brown flanks heaved in and out. At each outward breath, the membranous wings were pushed up, but they seemed to have no life of their own.

17

Lateef sat back on his heels and matched his breathing to the foal's. Then, tentatively, he reached over and touched one wing. It looked like a crumpled veil, silken-soft, and slightly slippery to the touch. Yet it was tougher than it looked. Lateef was reminded suddenly of the dancing women he had glimpsed going in and out of the Sheik's tent. They had that same soft toughness about them.

He touched the wing again. Then, holding it by the thin rib with one hand, he stretched it out as far as it would go. The wing unfolded like a leaf, and Lateef could see the dark brown veins running through it and feel the tiny knobs of bone. The foal gave a sudden soft grunt and at the same moment, Lateef felt the wing contract. He let it go and it snapped shut with a soft swishing sound.

"So," he said to the foal, "you *can* move the wing. You can shut it even if you cannot open it. That is good. But now I wonder: will you ever fly? Perhaps *that* is Allah's real test."

He stood up and looked around. All was sand. There was no difference between what was behind him and what was before. Yet he was a boy of the desert. He knew how to find directions from the traveling sun. Akbir lay to the north.

"Come, winged one," he said, bending down to lift the foal to his shoulders again. "Come, little brother. There is no way for us but north."

18

The foal made no noise as Lateef set out again. And except for Lateef's own breathing, the desert was silent. It drank up all sound. So, with the sand below, the sky above, and only the wind-sculpted dunes to break the unending horizon, Lateef walked on. He felt that he labored across a painted picture, so still was the land.

Then suddenly, rising up from the place where sand and sky meet, Lateef saw a great watery shape. First it was a beast, then a towered city, then an oasis surrounded by trees. The changes were slow, one image running into the next as a river is absorbed into the sea. Something in Lateef leaped with the sight and for a moment he let himself cry out in hope. But as the tears filled his eyes, Lateef reminded himself: "It is not a beast, not an oasis, not Akbir. It is only a mirage. Sun on the brain and sand in the eye." He spoke over his shoulder to the foal. "And I wonder what it is *you* see there, little brother." Then, closing his eyes and heart to the mocking vision, he trudged on, over the wind-scoured ripples, the changing, changeless designs on the desert floor.

When night came, he walked many miles farther under the light of the indifferent stars. Finally exhausted, he set his burden down and slept. But his sleep was fitful and full of dreams. He dreamed of sand, of sun, of stars. But he never once dreamed of the little horse that had curled against his chest, confident of the coming day.

19

THE CITY

Before dawn, before the sun could once more coax the shadow beasts and cloud cities to rise, Lateef set out again. He let the foal suck on the bottle and allowed himself a few sips as well. He dared not think about the coming heat or that his left foot had a cramp in it, or that his shoulders ached from the burdensome foal, or that his heart could not stop trembling with fear. He refused to let himself think about those things. Instead he thought about Akbir.

Akbir. His great-grandmother had been from Akbir. The daughter of a kitchenmaid, without a father to claim her, she had been sold into slavery. To the father of the father of Lateef's master, the Sheik. Lateef understood well that being the son of so many generations of slaves made him a person worth nothing. Less than nothing. Yet he dared to hope that, in Akbir, the home of his ancestors, he might change his position. With the foal as his touchstone, might he not even become a free man? A trainer of horses? An owner of stables?

He closed his eyes against the rising fantasy. Best, he cautioned himself, to think of only one thing at a time. Allah's jest or Allah's test. After all, he had no real idea what he would be able to do when he reached the pebbled streets, the mosaic mosques, the towered palaces of Akbir.

Walking forward quickly, his mind on the desert and not on his dreams, Lateef continued on. Even when he passed some horsemen at last and a caravan that jangled across his path for hours, he did not permit himself to dream. And in all that time, he spoke to no one other than the foal with whom he shared the wineskin.

But Lateef was not fooled into thinking that they had managed to come so far without the help of some unacknowledged miracle. After all, though he was an orphan, the great-grandson of a city dweller, he had been reared in the desert. His people had seventeen different words for sand, and not one of them was a compliment. He well knew that a solitary traveler could not hope to walk across the desert under the sun's unrelenting eye without more to stave off thirst than a single flask of mare's milk. And yet they had done so, the boy and the foal, and were alive as they finally stumbled onto one of the dirt-packed back streets of Akbir. Still, as if afraid of giving tongue to the word "miracle," as if speech might unmake it, Lateef remained silent. He set the foal down and then, as it stood, testing its wobbly legs against the ground, Lateef bowed down and kissed the road at the foal's feet.

The foal took a few steps down a road that led off to one side. Then it turned its head toward Lateef and whickered.

"Aiee, brother. That road it shall be," Lateef said. He caught up with the foal easily and gave it the last of the milk. Then he stroked its velvety nose and lifted it for one last ride upon his back.

Surprisingly there was no one in the street, nor in the roadways they crossed, nor in the *shook*, the marketplace, where stalls and stands carried handwork, and foodstuffs enough to feed a multitude.

21

Puzzling at this, Lateef explored further, passing from dirt roads to pebbled streets, from pebbled streets to roadways studded with colorful patterned stones.

The foal nuzzled his ear and at that moment Lateef heard a strange moaning. He turned and followed the sound until he came to a line of high walls. Standing in front of the walls were hundreds of people.

Women, dressed in black mourning robes, cried out and poured sand upon their heads. Men in black pants and ragged shirts wailed and tore at their own beards. Even the children, in their best clothes, rolled over and over in the roadway, sobbing. And the name that he heard on every lip was "Al-Mansur. Al-Mansur."

Lateef was amazed. He had never seen such extravagant grief. The dwellers of the desert, with whom he had lived all his life, were proud of their ability to endure tragedy and pain. Water, they said, was too precious to be wasted in tears. Their faces never showed hurt. That was why Lateef, who cried at another's pain and could not disguise his griefs, had been called "tender one" and despised by all.

As Lateef watched the wailing men and women and children, he felt tears start down his own cheeks. Embarrassed, he went over to one young mourner who was rolling in the street and stopped him gently with his foot.

"Tell me, city brother," said Lateef, "for whom do we weep?"

The boy looked up. "Oh, boy with horse shawl," he began, "we cry because our great king of kings, the Caliph Al-Mansur, is dying for want of a strange horse, a horse that he has seen only in his dreams. And though the Caliph is a man of mighty dreams, he has always before been able to have whatever he dreamed. Only this time he cannot. And none of our doctors, the greatest physicians in the world, can cure him. They cannot cure him for now he dreams of his death and, as it is written, there is no remedy for death." Then the boy fell back and pulled up some of the pebbles in the street, digging in the dirt beneath them. He covered his head with this dirt and began wailing again, this time louder than before.

"These are strange people," thought Lateef, "the people who dwell in cities. Yet I am of their blood. My great-grandmother was a sister to theirs. Surely that is why I am such a tender one. Still," he mused, "it is true that there is no remedy for death. I have heard that said many times in the desert. I have looked on many dead people, even in my short life, and have never known any of them to be cured."

And thinking about the Caliph's approaching death led him to think about the Caliph's dream. What could a man as rich and powerful as Al-Mansur desire so much that he might die of wanting? A horse, the boy said. But surely Al-Mansur could have any horse he wanted, any horse he dreamed of, any horse in his land.

"Perhaps the horse I carry is the very horse of the Caliph's dream," Lateef said to the weeping boy.

At his words, the boy stopped his noise and looked up. "That is no horse, but a rag around your shoulders. A rag on a rag. The Caliph is a great man, a giant. His dreams are big, too. He would laugh at such a jest should he see it." The boy began to laugh, but quickly the laugh turned back into a wail and he lay down again in the dust.

Lateef stroked the nose of the foal with one hand. "You are no jest to me, little brother," he said. Then he stepped over the wailing boy, pushed through the line of weeping people, and entered a gate in the wall.

Inside he saw the palace guards. They had taken off their great scimitars and, after laying the swords carefully on the ground, were rolling in the dirt and crying out their grief in tones even louder than the rest.

Lateef walked past them all and mounted the steps, marveling at the patterns on the stairs and walls. Behind him were the hundreds of grieving people. He wondered what lay ahead.

THE DREAM

Room upon room seemed to open before Lateef and he walked through each one as if in a dream. He, who had known only the tents of his Sheik, thinking them rich beyond his greatest imaginings, could not even begin to comprehend the wonders that belonged to the Caliph. The Sheik's desert tents now seemed but tattered remnants of an old beggar's cloak.

He followed a thread of sound, a wailing as thin and pure as a piece of spun gold. And when he found its beginning, he entered a room more splendid than any he had wandered in before.

Pearl-encrusted oil lamps sat on ebony tables. Draperies of wine-and-gold-colored silks hung on the walls. The wind of fifty fans held by fifty slaves made the shadows from the lamplight dance about the floor and over the carved faces of the wooden windowscreens.

In the center of the room was a mountain of pillows where a man lay, his head back and his bearded face bleached nearly as white as his robes and *dulband*. Only the red jewel of his turban had color. The ghost of his flesh hovered around his bones, for he had once been a large man, but was now shrunken with illness and age. His eyes were closed but his lips moved in and out as he breathed. Around him were seven weeping women dressed in veils, their noses and mouths covered but their eyes eloquent with tears. Four old men, wringing their hands and making sour mouths, listened by the bed.

As Lateef came closer, he could hear the man on the pillows speaking faintly.

"In my dream," the bearded man said, "I stood upon the brink of a river. I knew that I had to cross to the other side. But there was no boat to take me there and the waters were too wild and cold to swim. As I stood on the bank, longing for the other side, a wind began to dance around me. It blew sand in my face. I brushed my hand across my eyes to clear them and, when I could see once more, there was a great horse standing before me. The wind came from its huge shining wings fanning the air. I leaped onto its back. It pumped those mighty wings once, twice. Then, with a leap, it rose into the air. I looked below and the river was but a thin ribbon lying across a sandy vastness. I gave a great laugh, threw my hands above my head, and—laughing—fell from the horse and awoke again in my bed."

"It is the same dream, my Caliph," said the oldest man there, a man with a long white beard as fine as several silken threads.

"Of course it is," said the Caliph. "But if I do not find that horse, I will die." He sighed deeply and his stomach moved up and down.

The women began to wail again, but the old men shook their heads. The oldest spoke again.

"Be reasonable, my Caliph. To die for a dream?" he said.

"Is it better to die of old age? To die of a disease? I think," said

So the Caliph called the horse "Dragonfly." But Lateef did not.

"Brother," he named the foal. "Wind Brother." And he sang the name into the horse's ears and blew a breath gently into the foal's nostrils as was the custom among the desert dwellers. And he made the horse a song:

Wind rider,
Sun strider,
The dreamer's dream,

Moon leaper,
Star keeper,
Are you what you seem?

It was not a great song, but Lateef whispered it over and over in an affectionate tone as he touched the horse until it twitched its ears in reply. And the horse grew to love Lateef and would respond to his every command.

Often the Caliph would stand by the stall, holding on to the door for support while Lateef cleaned the horse. Or he would sit in a chair nearby while the horse's wings were stretched and rubbed with oil. But whenever the Caliph tried to come too close, both Lateef and the horse would tremble. Then the Caliph would sigh and a faint blush of color would stain his pale cheeks. "Ah, Dragonfly," Al-Mansur would say, "do not forget that you are my dream. And I must ride my dream or die."

One day, when Lateef and the horse had both trembled at the Caliph's approach, and Al-Mansur had sighed and spoken, Lateef could control his tongue no longer. Bowing low, afraid to raise his head, he spoke. "Oh Caliph, if what you say is so, then you are no more free than I."

The Caliph was silent for a moment, and when he spoke his voice was very soft. "No one is entirely free, child. Even I, Caliph Al-Mansur, have never been free to indulge my own dreams. To be good and wise, a ruler must make real the dreams of his people. But now, for once, I would have this dream, this wonder, for myself alone. For in some small way, the dreaming makes me feel I am free, though I know I am not."

Lateef shook his head, for he did not understand the Caliph. How could a man who had everything no further away than a handclap not be free? He raised his head to ask the Caliph, but the man was gone. He did not come again to the stable and his absence troubled Lateef.

When a year had passed and Wind Brother's sides had filled out, his mane and tail grown long and silky, the Caliph sent word around to the stables that he would come the very next day to ride the winged horse. Now in all this time, Wind Brother had never been mounted, nor had a saddle ever been placed upon his back. And never had he opened and shut his wings on his own. Lateef had been content to walk around the ring with the horse, his hand on Wind Brother's neck. He had feared that if he were to sit on the horse's back, his heels might accidentally do injury to the iridescent wings or that a saddle might crush a fragile rib.

Lateef bowed low to the messenger. "Tell my Caliph," he said fearfully, "and with many respects, that the horse is not yet strong enough for a rider."

The messenger looked even more afraid than Lateef. "I dare not deliver such a message myself. You must go."

So Lateef entered the Caliph's room for the second time. Al-Mansur lay on the silken pillows as if he were only dreaming of life.

"The horse, your . . . your Dragonfly," stuttered Lateef. "He is not yet ready to be ridden."

"Then make him so," said the Caliph, barely raising himself up to speak. He sank back quickly, exhausted from the effort.

Lateef started to protest but the guards hurried him out of the room. As he walked down the long hall, the Caliph's oldest adviser followed him.

"He *must* ride tomorrow," said the old man, his thin beard weaving fantastic patterns in the air as he spoke. "It is his only wish. He is growing weak. Perhaps it will keep him alive. A man is alive as long as he can dream."

"But *his* dream is of *my* horse."

"The horse is not yours, but the Caliph's. His grain has kept the horse alive. You are but a slave," said the old man, shaking his finger at Lateef. "A slave cannot own a horse."

"A slave can still be brother to the wind," Lateef whispered, aghast at his tongue's boldness, "as long as the wind wills it so." But even as he spoke, he feared he had failed—failed the horse and failed the Caliph—and in failing them both, failed himself.

ALLAH'S TEST

In the morning Lateef was up early. He rubbed the horse's sides with scented oils. He wove ribbons into its black mane. And all the while he crooned to the horse, "Oh, my brother, do not fail me as I fear I have failed you. Be humble. Take the Caliph onto your back. For you are young and healthy and he is old and sick. He is the dreamer and you are the dream."

The horse whickered softly and blew its warm breath on Lateef's neck.

Then Lateef took the horse out into the ring.

Soon the Caliph came, borne in a chair that was carried by four strong men. Behind them came the Caliph's advisers. Then, in order of their importance, came the Caliph's wives. Finally, led in by the armed guards, came the men and women and children of Akbir, for the word had gone out to the *shooks* and mosques: "Come see the Caliph Al-Mansur ride his dream."

Only then, when Lateef saw how many people waited and watched, did he truly become afraid. What would happen if the Caliph failed in front of all these people? Would they blame the horse for not bearing the Caliph's weight? Would they blame Lateef for not training the horse well? Or would they blame the Caliph? Failure, after all, was for slaves, not for rulers.

The Caliph was helped from his chair but then he signaled his people away. Slowly he approached the horse. Putting his hand to the horse's nose, he let Wind Brother smell him. He moved his hand carefully along the horse's flanks, touching the wings in a curious, tentative gesture, as if he had never really seen them clearly before. He spoke softly so that only the horse and Lateef could hear: "I am the dreamer, you are the dream. I think I am ready to ride."

Lateef waited.

The horse waited.

All the men and women and children of Akbir waited.

Suddenly, so swiftly it surprised them all, the Caliph took a deep breath and leaped onto the horse's back. He sat very tall on Wind Brother, his hands twisted in the horse's mane, his legs carefully in front of the wings. Eyes closed, the Caliph smiled and his smile was a child's, sweetly content.

For a long, breath-held moment, nothing happened. Then the horse gave a mighty shudder and reared back on his hind legs. He spun around and dropped onto all fours, arching his back. The Caliph, still smiling, flew into the air and landed heavily on the ground. He did not get up again.

The horse did not move, even when Lateef ran over to him and touched his nose, his neck, his side. But as Lateef swung himself astride, he felt the horse's flanks trembling.

"Be not afraid," Lateef whispered to the horse. "I am here. What they try to do to you, they must do to me first. In this I will not fail you."

The chief of the Caliph's guards ran toward the boy and the horse, his great silver scimitar raised above his head. As the scimitar began to sing its death song on the trip down through the air, Lateef leaned forward, guarding the horse's neck with his own. But he did not feel any blow. All he felt was a rush of wind as the horse began to pump its mighty wings for the first time.

Lateef turned his head. Above them he could still see the image of the silver sword. Then at his knee he felt a hand. He looked down. A boy about his own age stood there, in white robes, with a white *dulband* on his head. In the turban's center was the Caliph's red jewel.

"I am free and ready to ride," the boy said, a shadowy smile playing at the corners of his mouth.

"Then mount, my brother," whispered Lateef, putting his hand down and pulling the boy up behind him. "Ride your dream."

With a mighty motion, the horse's wings pumped once again, filling with air and sky. He lifted them beyond the sword, beyond the walls of the palace. They circled the minarets once and Lateef looked down. He could see a crowd gathering around the fallen figures of a Caliph, a horse, a ragged boy. Only here and there was a man or a woman or a child who dared to look up, who saw the dream-riders in the sky.

And then they were gone, the three: over a river that was a thin ribbon in the sand, over the changing patterns of the desert, to the place where there are neither slaves nor rulers and where all living beings truly dwell as brothers—the palace of the winds.

About the Author

Jane Yolen is the author of many distinguished books, including Dream Weaver, All in the Woodland Early, and How Beastly!. She teaches creative writing and is widely sought-after as a lecturer on folklore and children's literature. She and her family live on a farm in Massachusetts.

About the Artist

Barbara Berger's paintings have been exhibited extensively but this is her first book. A graduate of the University of Washington with a Fine Arts degree in painting, she now lives on an island near Seattle with several pets, including a mischievous rabbit.